There's Good All Around

TAMERA NORWOOD

ILLUSTRATED BY GRAZIELLA MILIGI

Small-Tooth-Dog Publishing
Tolleson, AZ

JUVENILE FICTION / Poetry
JUVENILE FICTION / Social Themes / Emotions & Feelings
Text by Tamera Norwood
Illustrations by Graziella Miligi
Formatting and interior design by Albatross Book Co.

Published 2021

The Small-Tooth-Dog Publishing Group
P.O. Box 392
Tolleson, Arizona 85353 USA
staff@smalltoothdog.com

Casebound ISBN 978-1-947408-34-0
Paperback ISBN 978-1-947408-33-3
Library of Congress Control Number: 2021943047

For lesson plans and resources, please visit: *www.tameranorwood.com*

For Braedon, Lili, Charlotte, and Elliott
who are good through and through.

Bad luck and bad news
can weigh your heart down,
but look, you will find,
there's good all around.

Goodness surrounds you
the moment you wake.
You're safe with your family
and friends that you make.

There are warm-hearted feelings
and babies so snug,
kisses to catch
and people to hug.

There are friends to be made
on buses, at school,
on playground equipment,
both ends of the pool.

There is time to play
in cardboard box forts,
treehouses, skate parks,
and basketball courts.

There's the care that you give
to pets of all kinds;
some that you raise
and some that you find.

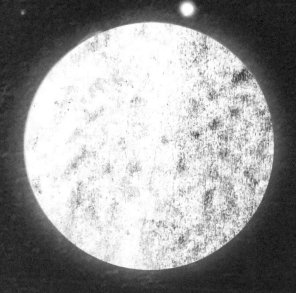

There are stars in the sky
and a sun that shines bright.
The moon always rises
to cast a nightlight.

There are moments of quiet:
the hush of snowfall,
books to get lost in
and dreams big and small.

There are songs in the seashells,
and bright, changing leaves,
the dance of cool raindrops,
a soft, scented breeze.

There are wonders in nature
where wildlife abounds,
in nests, hives, and burrows,
in pastures and mounds.

There are places to wander
through forests and parks,
campgrounds and beaches,
important landmarks.

There's so much to see:
the whole countryside,
mountains and deserts,
the ocean's blue tide.

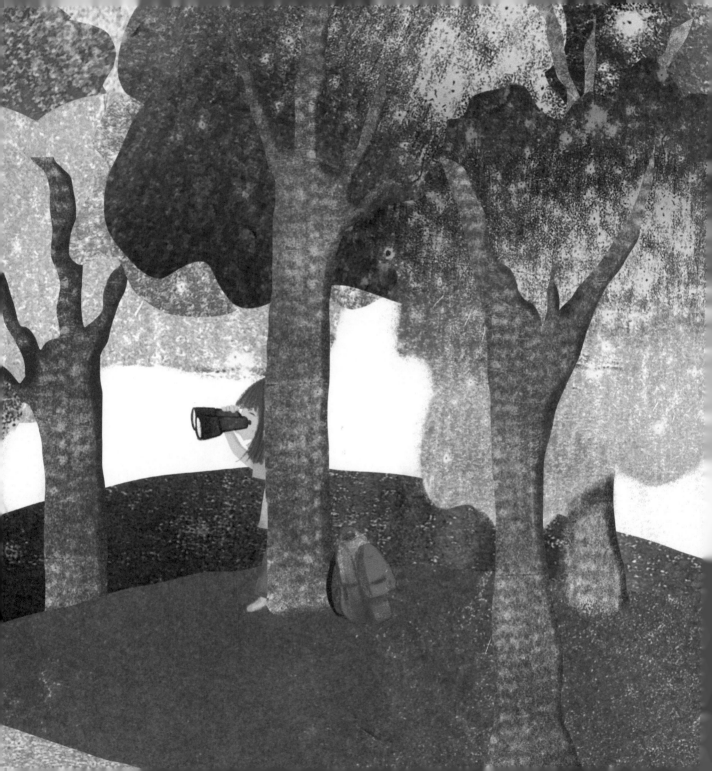

Bad moods and bad manners
can ruin your day.
But wait, you will see
those things fade away.

So many things
are good through and through.
There's good all around
and that includes you.

About the Author

TAMERA NORWOOD is a youth librarian who writes for pre-readers, young readers, and the adults who read to both.

She hopes to touch young hearts and make lifelong memories with her books.

Born and raised in the San Joaquin Valley of California, Tamera lives in Arizona with her husband and pets.

CPSIA information can be obtained
at www.ICGtesting.com
Printed in the USA
BVHW022008300921
617783BV00005B/136